HELLO, I'M THEA!

I'm *Geronimo Stilton's* sister. As I'm sure you know from my brother's bestselling novels, I'm a special correspondent for *The Rodent's Gazette*, Mouse Island's most famouse newspaper. Unlike my 'fraidy mouse brother, I absolutely adore traveling, having adventures, and meeting rodents from all around the world!

The adventure I want to tell you about begins at Mouseford Academy, the school I went to when I was a young mouseling. I had such a great experience there as a student that I came back to teach a journalism class.

When I returned as a grown mouse, I met five really special students: Colette, Nicky, Pamela, Paulina, and Violet. You could hardly imagine five more different mouselings, but they became great friends right away. And they liked me so much that they decided to name their group after me: the Thea Sisters! I was so touched by that, I decided to write about their adventures. So turn the page to read a fabumouse adventure about the

THEA SISTERS!

Colette

She has a passion for clothing and style, especially anything pink. When she grows up, she wants to be a fashion editor.

Paulina

Cheerful and kind, she loves traveling and meeting rodents from all over the world. She has a magic touch when it comes to technology.

Violet

She's the bookworm of the group, and she loves learning. She enjoys classical music and dreams of becoming a famouse violinist.

THE THEA SISTERS

Nicky

She comes from Australia and is very enthusiastic about sports and nature. She loves being outside and is always ready to get up and go!

Pamela

She is a great mechanic: Give her a screwdriver and she'll fix anything! She loves pizza, which she eats every day, and she loves to cook.

Do you want to help the Thea Sisters in this new adventure? It's not hard — just follow the clues!

When you see this magnifying glass, pay attention: It means there's an important clue on the page. Each time one appears, we'll review the clues so we don't miss anything.

**ARE YOU READY?
A NEW MYSTERY AWAITS!**

THE CAVE OF STARS

Scholastic Inc.

Copyright © 2018 by Mondadori Libri S.p.A. for PIEMME, Italy. International Rights © Atlantyca S.p.A., Via Leopardi 8, 20123 Milan, Italy; foreignrights@atlantyca.it, atlantyca.com. English translation © 2023 by Atlantyca S.p.A.

The publisher does not have any control over and does not assume any responsibility for author or third-party websites or their content.

Published by Scholastic Inc., *Publishers since 1920*, 557 Broadway, New York, NY 10012. SCHOLASTIC and associated logos are trademarks and/or registered trademarks of Scholastic Inc.

Stilton is the name of a famous English cheese. It is a registered trademark of the Stilton Cheesemakers' Association. For more information, go to stiltoncheese.co.uk.

This book is a work of fiction. Names, characters, places, and incidents are either the product of the author's imagination or are used fictitiously, and any resemblance to actual persons, living or dead, business establishments, events, or locales is entirely coincidental.

ISBN 978-1-338-84804-5

Text by Thea Stilton
Original title *La grotta delle stelle*
Art director: Iacopo Bruno
Cover by Barbara Pellizzari and Flavio Ferron
Illustrations by Giuseppe Facciotto, Barbara Pellizzari, and Flavio Ferron
Graphics by Marta Lorini

Special thanks to Becky Herrick
Translated by Andrea Schaffer
Interior design by Kay Petronio

10 9 8 7 6 5 4 3 2 1   23 24 25 26 27

Printed in China   38
First printing 2023

SURPRISE!

Nicky opened her eyes just before her ALARM
went off. She'd set it very early
because she wanted to go
for a run before getting
to work on the farm.

She immediately turned off the alarm and
carefully got out of the bunk bed, trying to
be as quiet as a mouse. But . . . CREAK!

The ladder groaned under her paw.

"Is it already time to get up?" mumbled her
friend Charlotte from the bunk below.

"Sorry, I didn't mean to wake you," Nicky
said. "I'm going *RUNNING*, but you can
still sleep for a bit!"

"Don't worry — I think I'll get up. I can
make a good breakfast!" Charlotte said.

Then she looked her friend in the eye and frowned. "Nicky, are you okay? You seem off."

"Nothing gets past you!" Nicky smiled. Charlotte was a new friend, but she was a

I'm going for a run....

What time is it?!

sensitive mouselet who'd quickly understood Nicky.

"I'm a little sad because my stay here is ending," Nicky said.

"Well, you can come back whenever you like. Consider the **BROWN FARM** your home in New Zealand!" Charlotte said. Her family owned the farm.

"I would love to come back here with my friends the THEA SISTERS," Nicky said with a dreamy smile.

Charlotte gave her a strange grin. "I think your WISH may come true — and maybe even sooner than you think!"

As Nicky left for her run, a light pink DAWN began to brighten the sky. The mouselet let her gaze wander over the green fields that surrounded the farm. Then she took a deep breath of fresh air and pumped herself up. "Time for a few more miles in **New Zealand**!"

When Nicky returned, the SUN was higher in the sky and the whole farm was awake. She slowed her pace to a quick walk, taking in every detail around her: the green grass, the fluffy coats of the **sheep** grazing nearby, the sounds of the cows that she knew by name, the smell of **EGGS** and **BEANS** that were

frying for breakfast, and the sparkling laugh of Charlotte, who appeared in the open kitchen window.

"I'll miss all of this," Nicky said to herself.

When she had decided to spend her break **working** on a New Zealand farm, she couldn't have imagined that six weeks would pass so quickly. And now just a pawful of days

New Zealand

New Zealand is an archipelago (group of islands) in the southeast Pacific Ocean. It is made of two large islands — the North Island, home to capital city Wellington, and the South Island — as well as many other small islands. While both islands have mountain ranges and forests, the South Island also has glaciers, sounds, fjords, and plains, while the North Island is warmer and has more sandy beaches, farmland, and an active volcanic and thermal area.

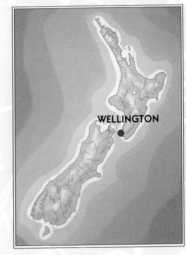

WELLINGTON

The islands were originally inhabited by the Māori, a Polynesian people who first arrived about a thousand years ago. Europeans sighted the land in the 1600s, and Great Britain annexed it as a colony in 1840. New Zealand has been independent since 1947 and is a member of the British Commonwealth. It currently has more than five million inhabitants, and while the majority are of European descent, there is a strong Māori culture still present.

were left until her return to **MOUSEFORD ACADEMY** on Whale Island.

I have so many things to tell my friends! Nicky said to herself. *I think about them so much that sometimes it seems like they're here. I can almost hear their* squeaks.

Just then Nicky heard a squeak from the kitchen. "And at that point, I told myself to calm down."

Great Gouda! That sounded just like . . .

"Colette! Don't exaggerate!" Nicky recognized Paulina's CHEERFUL squeak.

The mouselet stopped in her tracks. How could she hear the voices of her best friends from thousands of miles away?

TOGETHER AGAIN

Nicky peered uncertainly into the doorway of the kitchen, where BREAKFAST was being prepared. To her surprise, she saw her four favorite MOUSELETS there in the fur: Colette, Paulina, Pam, and Violet!

She closed her eyes. Was this her imagination? Was she so hungry that she was seeing things? Before she could open them, the Thea Sisters had surrounded her in a warm hug. "We missed you so much!" Pam shrieked, crushing Nicky in her arms.

"It's so **wonderful** to see you!" added Paulina.

"Tell us everything!" said Colette.

Nicky sputtered, "But . . . but . . . what are you doing here?!"

"Maybe you should ask Charlotte," Violet said with a smile.

The mouselet explained, "I noticed that you seemed to be a little DOWn lately, and I knew that only four mice in the world could really make you smile — so I invited them to visit New Zealand."

"Charlotte! This is the best GIFT you could have given me!" Nicky exclaimed tearfully.

"Sisters, I don't want to interrupt this moving moment," Pam said "But we don't want breakfast to get cold!" She pointed at a spread of eggs and beans, pancakes, toast covered with slices of caramelized banana, and bowls of yogurt and fruit.

Charlotte burst out laughing. "You're right, Pam. Let's eat!"

Breakfast is served!

Between mouthfuls, the mouselets updated Nicky on what had happened at Mouseford in the past few weeks, while she began to tell them about all the fabumouse disCoveries she'd made during her New Zealand experience.

When they were on their last bites, Charlotte clapped her paws and exclaimed, "Mouselets, are you ready for your first day on the farm?"

"Yes, we are!" Pam cried cheerfully.

"Are you sure?" Nicky winked.

"Of course!" squeaked Colette. "Animals . . . nature . . . It's all beautiful!"

"And **TIRING**," Nicky added. "The work here is wonderful, but it's also intense and exhausting!"

"Don't worry," Charlotte said. "We'll start with something light: Let's bring the sheep their breakfast!"

Charlotte and Nicky led the others to the barn that held the mother sheep and their little lambs. They were greeted by bleats. Nicky and Paulina changed their water, and Charlotte and the others took care of refilling the hay troughs.

"Look at that tiny lamb! It's adorable!" Colette said, approaching it. "Can I pet it?"

"Don't ask us — ask him!" said Nicky. "If he likes you, he'll let you **PET** him."

Colette gently reached her paw toward the

How cute!

little lamb's nose. He sniffed it suspiciously, then gave a soft BLEAT and let himself be petted.

"Great chunks of cheddar, these lambs are the cutest things I've ever seen!" Pam cried. "Coco, I'm coming to pet him, too!"

As she tried to make her way over between the sheep, though, Pam slipped and ended up in the hay. "OOPS!"

Oops!

"Pam, are you okay?" asked Nicky, giggling. "Luckily you fell on something soft!"

"Yeah, I'm fine," Pam said. "But there's something under here!" She pulled out a small metal box from under her leg.

"It looks like a CANDY TIN," Violet said, coming over to her friend. "What is it doing in the sheep barn?"

A DAY On THE FARm

The mouselets huddled around Pam.

"You're right, Violet, it's a tin of *MINTS*," Colette said, examining the box.

"Are those for the lambs' breath?" joked Pam.

Charlotte remained SERIOUS. "Nicky, remember that MOUSE Andy who stayed here for a night? He ate a lots of mints."

"He did!" Nicky replied. "He must have lost this tin, maybe when your father gave him a tour of the farm."

"Well, I don't think he would mind if I tried one," said Pam, taking the cover off the box.

On the iNSiDE, though, there were no mints — just a note!

"What's this?" Pam asked, grabbing it.

But . . . there are no mints!

Just then a sheep came up to her and tried to start **chewing** the paper!

"Um, let's leave the barn," Paulina said.

Back outside, the mice *PASSED* the note from paw to paw to read it.

The message said:

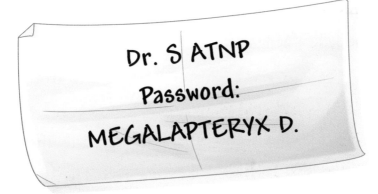

Dr. S ATNP

Password:

MEGALAPTERYX D.

"How strange! Is it some type of word game?" Colette wondered.

"It's sure a *tongue twister*," Pam said. "Megalapat . . . megalipta . . . oh, rats!"

Violet frowned and said, "Or it could be a message in code . . ."

BWAK, BWAK, BWAK!

"Uh-oh, someone else wants to eat breakfast!" Charlotte said cheerfully as clucking filled the air.

"And we certainly can't ignore them!" Nicky added. "Mouselets, let's forget about the MESSAGE for now and get to work. Okay?"

"Of course!" the others answered as they all headed to the chicken coop. The hens greeted them with a racket as they

SCRABBLED freely in their pen.

"Clearly, they're hungry!" Paulina smiled.

"And clearly, they're **NOT** perfumed," Colette said, wrinkling her snout.

"Oh, Coco!" Nicky chuckled. "It's just their **NATURAL** odor." While Charlotte passed out the feed, Nicky picked up a small **hen** with gold feathers and stroked her. "This is Dorothy. We've become friends!"

"Friends?" Colette asked.

"Yes! Come on, Coco, hold her! You probably ate some of her **eggs** at breakfast!"

"Er, I — well, I'm not very good with birds . . ." Colette mumbled, but then took the hen into her paws. "Oh, she's so warm and **SOFT**!"

Nicky smiled. "This is just one of the many happy surprises of farm life!"

Their day continued around the **farm**, where there was always something to do: a corner to organize, animals to look after, or plants to care for. They didn't realize how much time had passed until they heard **whistling** in the distance.

"That's my father returning from the pastures!" Charlotte said.

First to appear on the horizon was a magnificent **DOG** with black, white, and gold fur.

"Liam! **Good boy!**" Charlotte exclaimed, laughing as the dog **jumped** all over her and moved to greet Nicky.

"I see that our guests have arrived!" boomed

Mr. Brown. "Welcome to our farm!"

"We're so happy to be here!" Paulina
responded for everyone.

"Papa, have you gathered the **sheep**?" asked Charlotte.

"Of course — and did you take care of the ewes and lambs?" he replied.

"Yes, and also the hens, the orchard, and the barn. We've been **everywhere**!" responded Violet, smiling.

Mr. Brown chuckled. "I'm afraid your vacation here won't be very **relaxing**! Good thing you seem to be full of **ENERGY**."

"Actually, all this work has made me **incredibly** hungry!" Pam said, her stomach growling.

"You're in luck, because Papa is an amazing **COOK**!" Charlotte said. "And I bet he already has something great in mind for dinner. Right, Liam?"

The dog wagged his tail and let out a bark of approval.

Woof! Woof!

Pam laughed.

"I THINK HE'S HUNGRY, TOO!"

NIGHTTIME
DISCOVERIES

After a very big, fabumouse dinner of meat pie and baked fish, the four friends were exhausted.

Paulina yawned. "Cheese niblets! I'm so tired." she said. "I don't usually get sleepy so early."

MEAT PIE

A meat pie is made from puff pastry or pie dough that is stuffed with meat and other savory ingredients such as vegetables and cheese. Many different cultures around the world have their own version of this popular dish.

"I don't blame you for being tired," Nicky replied. She could see her friends were struggling to keep their eyes open. "I've gotten used to all this hard work in the open air, but my first days here were tough!"

"We'd better go to bed," Colette concluded. "Thanks for DINNER, Mr. Brown, and for the hospitality!"

"No, thank you for coming! Sleep well," Charlotte's father said. "Your adventure in New Zealand has just begun!"

Charlotte showed the new guests to their room, which had two bunk beds. "Nicky and I are in the room next door."

Soon the Thea Sisters were each under their COVERS. On the lower bunks, Paulina and Pam both conked out immediately. Colette skimmed the fashion news before putting her phone away. Just before going to sleep, she turned toward Violet, whose EYES were wide open.

"Vi, is everything okay?" Colette asked.

"I've been thinking about it all day . . ." Violet muttered.

Is everything okay?

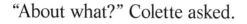
"About what?" Colette asked.

"*Megalapteryx*," responded Violet.

"Mega . . . what?!" Colette said. "Oh, you mean that *STRANGE* word on the note that Pam found this morning?"

Violet nodded. "It's actually a name, Coco. A Scientific name, to be precise. In fact, do you have your MousePhone handy?"

"Hold on . . ." Colette took out her **phone** and PASSED it to her friend, a little confused.

After a few seconds, Violet's face brightened. "Just as I thought! Look, here it is!"

She triumphantly turned the SCREEN to Colette. It showed an image of large bird with brown feathers that looked kind of like an **ostrich**.

"Mouselets, you woke me up!" Paulina complained. "What are you squeaking about?"

"Ask Violet! She's looking up pictures of strange ANIMALS," Colette responded.

"Are you feeling all right?" asked Pam, who had woken up, too.

"I think I know what that message in the box said, or at least part of it," Violet said. "**MEGALAPTERYX DIDINUS** was a bird from New Zealand!"

"Why *was*?" asked Paulina.

"Because it's been *extinct* for more than five hundred years," Violet explained.

"That's strange," Paulina whispered.

"We have to tell Nicky and Charlotte!" Colette cried.

"Sisters, can we do it in the morning?" Pam grumbled. "After **FIVE HUNDRED YEARS**, I don't think one more night will make much of a difference!"

Her friends laughed in agreement, and they all settled down for some much-deserved rest.

TRiP TO THE MOUSEUM

The next morning at breakfast, Violet was excited to share their **discovery** with Charlotte and Nicky.

"You see? This is a *Megalapteryx didinus*, also called the upland moa," she explained as she finished her bowl of yogurt and fruit.

Charlotte looked at the **image** on her friend's phone and commented, "I've seen this bird in some books. Actually, I think I've seen one of these in real life!"

"Moldy mozzarella, that's impossible!" Pam cried. "It's been extinct for **centuries.**"

Charlotte shook her snout. "I don't mean I've seen one alive in the fur — I've seen a

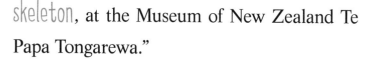
skeleton, at the Museum of New Zealand Te Papa Tongarewa."

"Really?!" said Paulina. "I'd love to see it!"

"We could go over to the **mouseum** today if you'd like," Charlotte proposed. "It's in Wellington, not far from here."

"But what about the **work** on the farm?" asked Colette.

Nicky explained, "Charlotte and her father have given us all a day off to be tourists and to **visit** the area!"

"Oh!" Colette said in surprise.

"Don't worry, Coco — you can see your friend Dorothy tomorrow," teased Paulina.

"A visit to the mouseum is a fabumouse idea for our free day!" Violet said. "And maybe we can learn more about that strange message we found."

"Let's do it!" agreed Nicky.

Not long after, the Thea Sisters came outside, ready to head to the mouseum.

"Charlotte said to wait for her here. She must be getting the *CAR*," Paulina said.

Nicky smiled. "It's not exactly a car . . ."

"What do you mean —"

BEEP! BEEEEEP!

The sound of a horn made the mouselets jump. There was Charlotte, driving an RV painted with big, colorful flowers!

"Sweet cheese on a stick! Now that is a fabumouse **CAMPER**!" Pam said, giving it a pat.

"Hop in!" Charlotte squeaked.

The drive to the city took a little over an hour. The mouselets filled the time chattering and admiring the landscape scrolling by.

"Welcome to Wellington, the capital of New Zealand!" Charlotte announced. "And here's Te Papa, our destination. It's full of artifacts and works of art that trace the entire history and culture of our country. I've visited it many times in my life!"

"I can't wait to check it out!" Violet exclaimed.

"Where did the mouseum get its NAME?" Paulina wondered.

"It's a MĀORI name — the Māori are the original inhabitants of New Zealand," Charlotte replied as she parked the RV. "*Te Papa Tongarewa* translates to 'container of treasures,' which describes the mouseum well!"

The mouselets went in and began browsing.

"Sisters, this is amazing!" Pam squeaked, pointing up at an enormouse structure decorated with masks and colored sculptures.

"It's called **Te Marae**," Charlotte explained. "It's a Māori communal meeting place, with carved ancestral images."

"Wow!" the Thea Sisters squeaked as they admired its beauty.

Then Violet said, "It's beautiful, but we haven't yet seen the *Megalapteryx* skeleton. Do you remember where it is, Charlotte?"

Her friend nodded. "It's in the Nature exhibition. Come with me!"

Charlotte led them to a large space that held skeletons and preserved pieces of many ancient animals. But there was no trace of the *Megalapteryx*.

"Are you sure this is where you saw it?" asked Nicky.

"Yes, it definitely should be in here," Charlotte confirmed.

"Why don't we ask a GUiDe?" Nicky proposed. "There's one!"

Nicky approached a ratlet standing next to an artifact. He had a mouseum badge on his shirt.

How spectacular!

Where is the skeleton?

"Excuse me, could you please give us a paw?" she said. "We're looking for a skeleton . . ."

"You've come to the right place," he responded with a smile. "I'm Tāmati. How can I help you?"

"I was sure there was a skeleton of an **UPLAND MOA** in here," Charlotte said as she came over. "But I can't find it!"

Could you give us a paw?

The broad smile on Tāmati's snout faded. "Unfortunately, it's not here anymore."

"Did they **TRANSFER** it to another mouseum?" asked Charlotte, surprised.

Tāmati responded, "The truth is . . . it was stolen."

"**Stolen?!**" Nicky exclaimed. "Cheese and crackers! Who would steal a skeleton?!"

"This wasn't just any old skeleton — it's an ancient artifact that was well preserved," Tāmati said. "The rodent who stole it was very **CLEVER**. The mouseum has set a reward for whoever finds it."

He showed the mouselets a flyer with a **PHOTO** of the skeleton and the notice of the reward. They all stood there in silence for a moment.

"Has it been missing long?" Violet asked.

"It's only been a week," Tāmati responded.

"Charlotte, when did that **RAT** stay at the farm?" Violet asked immediately.

"Who? Oh, of course, Andy . . . well, I think it was about a week ago, right, Nicky?"

Nicky nodded. "Yes. He arrived at night and asked to stay. All he had with him was that tin of MINTS and a large bag with a logo of an anchor and two fish on it."

Charlotte nodded and said, "Papa insisted on taking him on a tour of the farm, even though it was late. And he left very early the next morning, without having breakfast or saying good-bye."

"Ahem . . ." Tāmati cut in. "Could you tell me what you're squeaking about?"

Charlotte explained, "We didn't just come here to visit the mouseum: We found a strange note with the word Megalapteryx on it, which seemed like some type of code or clue."

"But maybe there's something more behind it," Violet said. "The rat who lost the note could be INVOLVED in the disappearance of the skeleton!"

CLUE!

A MYSTERIOUS VISITOR TO THE FARM LEFT BEHIND A NOTE MENTIONING MEGALAPTERYX RIGHT AROUND THE TIME THE SKELETON WAS STOLEN FROM THE MOUSEUM. IS THAT MOUSE CONNECTED WITH THE THEFT?

A NEW CLUE

Charlotte and the Thea Sisters all started talking at once, and Tāmati suggested they find a better place to **discuss** the situation. He led them just outside the museum to a nice **CAFÉ** with wooden tables and stools. The group sat down, and Charlotte ordered fruit juice for everyone.

"So you met a rat who might have **stolen** Didi?" Tāmati said.

"Wait, who is Didi?" asked Colette.

"Didi, as in *didinus*?" Violet asked. "Did you give a **NICKNAME** to a skeleton?"

Tāmati blushed to the roots of his fur. "You know, I'm at the mouseum every day, both as a guide and for my art studies, and . . . well, I was **FOND** of the upland moa!"

"That's why you're so interested in our suspicions," Nicky said, smiling.

"There's actually another reason," Tāmati admitted. "I come from Rotorua —"

We must figure out what happened!

"The city famouse for its thermal baths and MĀORI culture?" Paulina interrupted him.

Tāmati nodded. "Yes! I haven't lived there for many years. I miss it very much. My dream is to open a SCHOOL of art and design there for the mouselings in the area. If I can get the reward that the mouseum promised for the skeleton, my dream could come true."

The mouselets then explained their situation to Tāmati: how, a week ago, when the robbery took place, there was also **mysterious** guest named Andy at Brown Farm. He'd dropped a tin of mints there that contained a note that seemed like a message in code.

"Pam, do you have the TIN so we can show it to Tāmati?" asked Nicky.

"You bet your Brie I do! It's in my pocket,"

said Pam, placing the mint tin on the table. She opened it with a click. "Here is the note —

oOOPS!"

The box slid toward the edge of the table.

"**GOT IT!**" Charlotte squeaked, then looked closely at the tin in her paw. "There's something else stuck in the bottom here. Look!" She pulled out a second folded **paper.** It was a PHOTO of a mouse in a white coat.

"How strange! Is that the rat that you hosted?" asked Pam.

Nicky shook her snout. "It's not him."

"Hold on!" exclaimed Violet. "That looks like a doctor's coat. What if this mouse is the doctor that the note from the tin talks about?"

"Now we're cooking with **CHEESE**! I bet this is Dr. Satnp!" Pam said.

Violet looked closely at the photo. "Hmm . . . he has a **TAG** on his coat, but I can't read what it says."

"I have an idea!" Paulina said. She took her **TABLET** from her purse and photographed the image. She enlarged and enhanced it until they could read the words on the tag. It said: National Parks.

"This Dr. Satnp could be a scientist who works for the national parks of New Zealand," Violet said.

"But how is he related to Andy?" asked Charlotte.

Everyone thought for a moment until Tāmati exclaimed, "Wait a second!" The mouselets all stared at him, and he continued. "It isn't Dr. Satnp — it's Dr. S, and then the initials **ATNP**, which are an acronym for Abel Tasman National Park!"

"It must be a scientist who works for that park," Violet said.

"Do you know where it is?" asked Nicky, turning to Charlotte and Tāmati. "Can we go there?"

"Well, yes, but we'll have to travel pretty far, including over a stretch of sea. So it'll take time, and we'd need somewhere to stay overnight," Tāmati responded.

The mouselets **SMILED**. Charlotte said, "It just so happens that neither the distance nor the night is a **problem** for us!"

CLUE!

DOES THE PHOTO SHOW THE DR. S REFERENCED IN THE NOTE? AND DOES HE HAVE SOMETHING TO DO WITH THE STOLEN MEGALAPTERYX SKELETON?

A BREAK BETWEEN THE WAVES

The mice headed to the **CAMPER**, and Charlotte proposed a plan. "We can get on the road immediately and sleep in the RV when we arrive near the park," she said. "Tomorrow morning, we can get up early to **search** for clues."

Tāmati smiled wistfully. "That seems like a great plan. Abel Tasman is a wonderful park, and it would be fantastic if you discovered more about Didi's disappearance!"

"Why don't you come with us?" Nicky asked eagerly. "You care even more than we do about what happened to your friend Didi."

"Well, I do have a few days off, and it's been a while since I took a trip. But I don't want to be too much trouble," he replied.

"Nonsense! Everyone hop in — I'll just call my dad to let him know, and we'll be off!" Charlotte said cheerfully.

And so the mouselets and their new friend set out for the South Island.

Paulina read aloud from info on the internet as they drove. "Here it says that Abel Tasman is the smallest national park in New Zealand," she said. "You can visit it on paw, by boat or kayak, or —"

"By kayak? Wow, fabumouse!" exclaimed Nicky. "I would love to try that . . ."

"It would be fun, but we're on a MISSION!" Violet pointed out.

The next morning, after the **night** in the camper, the group went to the visitor center in Mārahau, a town right by the park. They hoped to find the scientist from the photo there. Unfortunately, the center was closed for the next few hours.

"Rancid ricotta! We'll have to **WAIT**," Paulina said.

"I have a better idea!" Tāmati said. "What do you say we take advantage of this time by going on an excursion? We're in one of the most beautiful parks in *New Zealand*, after all!"

"Great idea!" Pam cried. "Let's go exploring!"

As the mice walked into the park, a **SPECTACULAR** landscape unfolded

before them. The forest glittered with a thousand SHADES of green in the clear light of the morning.

With every step, the friends seemed to enter further into an enchanted world among the fresh scents of plants and **sounds** of animals.

"Hey, look down there!" yelled Pam, pointing at a bird on the edge of the trail.

"That's a pukeko," explained Tāmati. "You can recognize it by its dark feathers and its red beak!"

The friends explored the park for the next few hours. Every step led them to discover a new natural wonder! But none of it was useful to their investigation of the stolen skeleton. They ended up at a **kayak** rental spot on a beach.

"Crusty cheese chunks! This place is incredible!" Pam shouted, gazing at the golden sand lapped by clear blue water.

"This park is famouse for its beaches!" Tāmati said. "Looks like we still have some time — we could grant Nicky's wish for a kayak ride. What do you say?"

In response, Charlotte scurried right over to the rental counter. It didn't take long for the friends to each get set up with a boat and LIFE JACKETS.

The elderly rodent who owned the rental agency gave them lots of kayaking tips, and finally, the mice entered the water. They already had experience with canoes, and soon they were gliding **peacefully** around the park's coast.

Under the splendid sun, everyone briefly forgot their MISSION and dedicated themselves to rowing and enjoying the beauty around them.

Suddenly, Nicky pointed ahead of them and exclaimed, "Look!"

A large, DARK MASS was moving through the crystal water, slowly approaching Paulina's and Colette's kayaks.

"SQUEEEAAAAK!" yelled Colette. "What is that thing?!"

The animal flicked its tail, splashing the kayak, then dove down again.

Charlotte burst out laughing. "You just met one of the most famouse residents of the park . . . a seal!"

Tāmati explained, "We're near an island

where different colonies of seals live. If we're *lucky*, we will even see some —"

"*Pups!*" yelled Nicky. "Right there!"

A group of seals and their pups were lying on some rocks by the water.

"How wonderful!" Violet said.

The mice paddled slowly, making sure to not get too close to the animals in their habitat. Eventually, Tāmati said, "I think it might be time to go back. This has been a lovely excursion, but . . ."

"We don't want to *forget* Didi!" Nicky agreed with a smile.

ONE WRONG
DELIVERY

Their journey out of the park was much **FASTER** than the way in.

"The visitor center must be open by now," Violet said. "Let's hope we can find more information about that **doctor**!"

"We made it!" Paulina said, pointing at an office **BUILDING** ahead.

They went inside. The lobby was full of park employees and visitors scurrying around looking for information.

"I don't see anyone who looks like him," Pam said, checking the **PHOTO** of the doctor.

Where is Dr. S?

"Can I have that for a second, Pam?" Colette asked. Photo in her paw, she went up to a desk where a ratlet sat working at a **computer**.

"Excuse me, do you know if the rodent in this photo works here?" Colette asked politely.

The ratlet lifted his gaze for a moment, then said, "Sinclair? Third door down the hallway."

Do you know this rodent?

"Oh, thank you!" Colette responded, a little surprised. She went back to her friends with a smile. "We hit the Jack-cheese-pot! The rat in the photo is Dr. Sinclair, and his office is down the hall!"

"**Fabumouse!**" Pam said. "Let's go there now!"

"Well . . ." Charlotte cleared her throat. "I'm not sure that seven of us should swoop into a stranger's office to ask him why his photo was inside a tin of mints in my barn. That might scare him off."

"Fair point," Nicky said. "Maybe just you and I could go in. What do you mice think?"

"We'll wait for you here!" Pam replied for everyone.

Nicky and Charlotte went down the

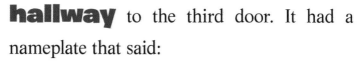

hallway to the third door. It had a nameplate that said:

DR. H. SINCLAIR

Nicky took a breath and knocked, but no one responded.

"I don't think **anyone** is here," Charlotte said. "Maybe we should —"

Just then a delivery mouse approached the two friends with a box in his paws.

"You're Dr. Sinclair's assistants, right?" he said. "I have a package for him, and I'm very late. Please get this to him. Goodbye!" Then he shoved the PACKAGE into Nicky's paws and scampered off before they could squeak.

"Wait — we aren't . . ." Nicky began to say, but the mouse had already disappeared.

"Let's bring the box to the reception desk," Charlotte said. "They can figure out how to get it to the doctor."

Nicky nodded and studied the package as they started to walk back. "It looks like a large box of **CHOCOLATES** —" Suddenly, she stopped in her tracks, then said, "Great Gouda! Charlotte, read this!"

A **NOTE** was stapled to the box:

Now every little bone is in its place. Thanks. When you want to take a trip to the glowworms, you will be welcome! —A.

"Are you thinking what I am thinking?!" Charlotte said after READING it.

Nicky nodded. "'Every little bone is in its

place' could refer to the stolen *Megalapteryx* skeleton!"

"And 'A.' could be for Andy, the **RAT** who stayed at the farm!" continued Charlotte. "We've got to tell the others!"

MAKE LiKE A CHEESE WHEEL!

Nicky and Charlotte left the for the doctor at the reception desk, then joined their friends. On the way back to their RV, they filled the others in about the note they'd seen.

"Maybe we're on the right track," Violet said. "What if Andy had an appointment with Dr. Sinclair and wrote down info about it in code so no one else could understand it? Then he printed a photo of the doctor so he would recognize him and hid that and the note in the tin of mints."

"And then he lost it!" Paulina said.

Violet nodded. "Then they must have met up, and now Andy has sent Dr. Sinclair a box

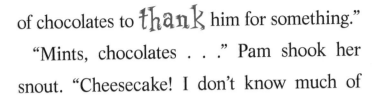

of chocolates to thank him for something."

"Mints, chocolates . . ." Pam shook her snout. "Cheesecake! I don't know much of

Maybe this is what happened . . .

what's happening other than that this rat has a big sweet tooth!"

Tāmati chuckled, but Nicky sighed. "Why did Andy meet up with Dr. Sinclair?"

"If Andy stole the skeleton, Dr. Sinclair might have helped him," Violet said.

"Yeah!" Paulina agreed. "Maybe he gave Andy advice on how to store it without damaging it."

"It's still unclear," Tāmati said, "But at least now we have a new lead: the GLOWWORMS!"

"Too bad that's such a strange clue," Paulina said. "Glowworms? Who knows what he meant by that!"

"He meant actual GLOWING WORMS," Tāmati replied with a smile. The Thea Sisters looked confused, so he went on. "Here in

New Zealand, there are creatures that live in humid, **DARK** caves, and they are able to produce light. They're called glowworms in English, but in the language of my people, the Māori, they are called titiwai, which means 'lights reflected in water.'"

"**COOL!**" Paulina exclaimed.

Tāmati smiled. "And there's a famouse place where they can be found . . ."

"Of course!" Charlotte cried. "How did I not think of it before? Waitomo!" She explained, "It's a place on the North Island, quite far from here, known for its glowworm **CAVES**. Come on, friends, let's make like a cheese wheel and roll!"

LET'S REVIEW THE CLUES!

A PRIZED SKELETON WAS STOLEN FROM THE MOUSEUM RIGHT AROUND THE TIME A MOUSE NAMED ANDY STAYED OVERNIGHT AT THE BROWN FARM WITH A LARGE BAG IN TOW.

THE THEA SISTERS FOUND A NOTE INSIDE A MINT TIN ANDY LEFT BEHIND THAT MENTIONED DR. S AND THE MEGALAPTERYX.

ANDY SENT DR. SINCLAIR CHOCOLATES TO THANK HIM FOR SOMETHING.

THERE WAS A NOTE ON THE CHOCOLATES THAT INVITED THE DOCTOR TO VISIT WAITOMO.

A CAVE OF STARS

It was a very **long** drive to Waitomo: hundreds of miles, including a short stretch by **FERRY** back to the North Island. The mice took their time driving, and they arrived at the gates of Waitomo very late at night.

"Having a **CAMPER** is amazing," Pam said. "It's like a portable house with everything you need!"

"The best part is that it can be a portable bedroom! **YAWN!**" Violet added. "I don't know about you, but I'm wiped!"

Tāmati parked the RV. "Let's stay here for the **night** and start our search for Andy in the morning."

"Agreed," Nicky responded. "Tomorrow we'll get up early and make a **PLAN**!"

But the mice were exhausted after such an intense day of travel. When Charlotte's cell phone **ALARM** rang, she turned it off without waking, and everyone slept in.

Once Colette opened her eyes and looked at her watch, it was already past nine.

"Squeeeak! We overslept!" she cried.

"Huh? What? How?" mumbled Pam. She jumped out of bed, banging her head against the ceiling of the camper. "Ouch!"

"It's time to go look for Andy!" Colette said, shaking Violet **AWAKE**. Soon everyone was up.

"Where do we begin?" asked Nicky.

"I would say at the glowworm **CAVES**," said Tāmati. "It's the **ONLY** lead that we have!"

The mice soon reached the entrance to the cave tours. It was crowded with visitors.

Charlotte *GASPED* and pointed at a rodent standing on a boat full of tourists that was slowly moving toward the caves. "Nicky, isn't that . . . ?"

"Andy!" Nicky finished, recognizing the rat who'd been at the farm. "It's definitely him. It looks like he's a **GUIDE** to that group. Let's follow them!"

The friends all *JUMPED* into a boat that was waiting at the dock and asked to depart immediately. But their guide firmly shook her snout. "I'm afraid that's not possible. We have to wait twelve minutes: The tours are organized according to a fixed **SCHEDULE** so that the caves don't fill with too many visitors at once. But you'll see — the time will pass in the twitch of a

WHISKER and it will be worth the wait!"

The mouselets **SIGHED**. They were so close to Andy, but they'd have to wait.

When their boat finally departed, though, the mice could hardly believe their eyes!

The small **boat** glided silently through the dark water. Above them was a luminous vault of glowworms, their blue lights more intense than a starry sky.

"It's so beautiful," whispered Violet happily. "It feels like a dream."

Paulina held up her paw in silence, her heart full.

Soon, though, the group emerged from the EXTRAORDINARY cave and returned to reality and their mission.

"There's Andy," Charlotte said, pointing

ahead toward the exit of the tour. "He's going outside with those tourists."

"Let's not lose **sight** of him!" Paulina said.

The friends got off the boat onto a small dock and finally caught up with the mysterious mouse they'd been chasing.

SNOUT TO SNOUT

Charlotte tapped Andy's shoulder. "Excuse me."

He turned and said with a smile, "Yes? Do you need something?"

Then he seemed to recognize her. For a fraction of a second, his smile wavered, but it immediately returned.

"Do you remember me?" Charlotte asked. "You stayed at my family's farm — the **BROWN FARM**, near Wellington — not long ago."

"Oh, yes, of course," Andy said. "Thanks again for the hospitality. Are you on vacation here at Waitomo?"

Nicky stepped forward and said, "Actually, we came here to LOOK for you. These are yours, right?" She held out the note and the **PHOTO** of Sinclair.

"How did you get those?!" Andy exclaimed, caught off guard.

We found these!

"We found them at the farm, inside a **TIN** of mints that you must have lost," Charlotte said. "We figured out who **Dr. Sinclair** was, and that you two are hiding —"

A loud laugh cut off her squeak.

"**На, на, на!** So you found our wordplay, huh?" Andy said.

The friends looked at one another in confusion. Was their **suspect** confessing?

But Andy went on. "Sinclair and I have known each other for many years, practically forever. We went to school together as mouselings not far from here, and since then, we have fun by sending each other little puzzles or puns, usually about fossils, which we're both interested in!"

"Puzzles? Wordplay?" repeated Charlotte, confused.

Andy nodded. "You see, Sinclair was telling me about a meeting, but in code."

"What about the Megalapteryx reference?" asked Colette.

"It was the answer to a riddle I'd sent!" Andy chuckled. "Thanks for bringing these back to me. I hope you didn't come all the way here for just this, though!"

"Andy! Come on — there's a new group," the **GUIDE** from the boat the friends had been on called over.

"I'm afraid I have to go," Andy said.

"Wait!" Nicky stopped him. "When you stayed at the Brown Farm, you had a bag with you that seemed really heavy. What was in it?"

"My keyboard," he said quickly.

"Andy, are you coming?" said the other guide, coming up to them.

"Hey, Carla," he said to her, "I'm a great keyboard player, aren't I?"

Carla smiled. "Well, I guess you're not bad at it . . . but you're definitely not very modest!"

Andy smirked at the Thea Sisters and their

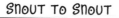
friends, and said, "Sorry — duty calls. It was a pleasure to meet you! Good-bye!"

He scurried off, leaving the friends **confused**.

"Cheese niblets! Is it possible that we've made a big MISTAKE?" Paulina wondered.

Nicky sighed and said, "I'm afraid so!"

THE INVESTIGATION BEGINS AGAIN!

The mice were disappointed as they headed back to the RV.

"I guess we should just head back to the farm," Charlotte said.

"What a pity," Colette murmured.

Violet was as lost in her thoughts as a rat in a maze.

Nicky added, "I'm sorry we didn't find any information about Didi, Tāmati. I really thought that . . . Tāmati?!"

Her friend had stopped and was touching his neck with alarm.

"Are you okay?" Pam asked.

Tāmati shook his snout. "I think I LOST my

*hei matau!** I'll be right back, I have to find it."

Then he turned and scurried away. Nicky explained to the other Thea Sisters, "A hei matau is a Māori pendant necklace," she said. "I saw that Tāmati wore one."

"I noticed it, too!" Colette said. "It was a beautiful green stone that was shaped like a fishhook."

Nicky nodded. "I'm sure it's very important to him. Let's hope he can find it!"

"Mouselets, should we all go help him look for it?" Charlotte asked.

Just then Tāmati finally reappeared. He had a strange light in his eyes.

*A stone pendant carved in the shape of a fishhook, made by the Māori. They are said to bring the wearer strength and safety while traveling at sea.

"From your expression, I think you found your pendant," Colette said cheerfully.

Tāmati nodded. "And more! I heard something very, very interesting . . ."

The ratlet told them how he had retraced his steps and seen the hei matau **WEDGED** between some rocks by the path. When he kneeled to pick it up, he heard Andy's squeak on a PHONE CALL right behind him. Andy was saying, "I had a small problem with a few annoying mice . . . but everything should go as planned tomorrow at Bayswater!"

"It seems that Andy really does have something to hide after all," Nicky said.

"I thought so!" Violet added. "His EXPLANATIONS about the note didn't convince me at all. Think about it:

Sinclair is the doctor's last name, not his first name. Who calls a dear childhood friend only by his **LAST NAME**?"

"So Andy lied about his friendship with the doctor?" asked Colette.

"I think so," Violet said.

Then Paulina took out her tablet and said, "We can try to verify it. I'll look for Dr. Sinclair's bio — just a minute."

Soon Paulina said, "Here it is!"

"Look, he only arrived in New Zealand five years ago — before that he was in Melbourne, Australia!" she cried.

DR. HENRY SINCLAIR

BORN IN MELBOURNE, AUSTRALIA

PHD IN BIOLOGY AND ZOOLOGY FROM UNIVERSITY OF MELBOURNE

ACTIVE IN NEW ZEALAND FOR THE PAST FIVE YEARS

"I knew it!" Violet squeaked. "He wasn't Andy's childhood friend in New Zealand. His whole story about riddles was just **INVENTED** to fool us."

"He must be **HIDING** something!" Charlotte exclaimed. "He and Dr. Sinclair must be working together!"

"Which means that our investigation is still open!" Nicky concluded.

CLUE!

DID ANDY INVENT THE STORY OF HIS CHILDHOOD FRIENDSHIP WITH DR. SINCLAIR TO TRY TO HIDE THEIR CRIME?

WHERE DID ANDY GO?

The Thea Sisters, Charlotte, and Tāmati knew what they had to do next: find Andy. This time, they wouldn't leave him in peace until he confessed everything he knew about the missing skeleton.

"Let's split up and look for him!" Nicky proposed. "Tāmati and I will go back to the GLOWWORM cave, and you mice can divide up and search the other caves in the area!"

"I'm sure we'll find him faster than the mouse ran up the clock!" Pam said.

But her optimism soon vanished.

"We didn't see him at all," Paulina said when she and Colette returned.

"He wasn't on the **TRAILS** we searched," Charlotte added. She, Violet, and Pam had looked in every corner.

Nicky and Tāmati couldn't find him, either. "There's no **TRACE** of Andy. It's like he evaporated!" Nicky complained.

"Did he **sneak** off?" Paulina wondered.

"One thing is for sure," Charlotte said. "If we could squeak with Andy again, we'd have a bunch of questions to ask him . . ."

Just then they heard a female squeak. "I know where you can find him!"

"Carla!" Colette was surprised to see the guide who had led them on the boat tour.

"**Hi!** Do you still have some questions?" she asked in a friendly tone. "If you want to talk to Andy, you can find him at the café nearby. Just walk down the main road toward Hangatiki."

"Are you sure we'll **find** him there?" asked Charlotte.

Carla nodded. "When he finishes work, he always goes there for some hokey pokey!"

We're looking for Andy . . .

He'll be eating ice cream!

"Perfect. Thank you!" Nicky said, and she and her friends scurried down the road at a quick pace.

"Excuse me, what is *hokey pokey?*" Pam asked.

"It's a type of ice cream," Charlotte explained.

"Oh!" Pam's snout lit up. "I want to try that!"

"If we find Didi, I will buy you all the hokey pokey you want!" Tāmati replied.

HOKEY POKEY

One of the most popular ice-cream flavors in New Zealand is called hokey pokey. It's vanilla ice cream with pieces of honeycomb candy mixed in.

Colette giggled. "Be careful, friend — you don't know what you're promising! Pam **LOVES** ice cream almost as much as cheese!"

"We're here!" Nicky interrupted them, pointing at a café ahead. "Let's go in!"

"I don't know if we need to," Charlotte said. "Look!"

Andy was right by one of the large open windows, eating a big bowl of ice cream at a table with another mouse.

They were relaxed, laughing and chatting — they seemed to simply be two friends meeting up for a SNACK.

The Thea Sisters were a bit disoriented by this scene. Paulina commented, "I guess Andy didn't sneak off to hide a skeleton."

"Instead, he just went to have a snack — something that I'd also like to do!" added Pam, massaging her stomach.

"It's very *strange*," Violet said.

Nicky continued. "Either Andy is reckless, or he's not **AFRAID** that we'll find out, or —"

"Or he doesn't have any skeletons to hide," Violet said thoughtfully.

THE LAST CLUE

At that, everyone turned toward Violet.

"Vi, what are you saying? Andy **LIED** about his friendship with Dr. Sinclair to explain the notes, and he was clearly **annoyed** that we might interfere with his plans!" Colette exclaimed.

"It's clear he stole the skeleton!" Nicky added.

Think about it . . .

But Violet shook her snout. "If you had stolen a **PRECIOUS** artifact and were trying to keep it hidden somewhere, and a group of nosy mice arrived asking you questions, would you be **CALMLY** eating ice cream as usual, where it would be easy for anyone to find you?"

"Well, maybe he didn't take us seriously," Charlotte said.

But Paulina agreed with Violet. "It doesn't really make sense. If Andy stole the skeleton, why did he go back to being a **guide** at Waitomo as if nothing had happened?"

"Maybe he got rid of it," Tāmati suggested.

"Exactly!" Violet replied. "I think that Andy stole it and then gave it to someone else: the rodent he was on the phone with when Tāmati overheard him."

Tāmati frowned. "If that's the case, I have good and bad news. The good news is that we have a lead, which is the place that I heard him squeak: Bayswater. The bad news is that it's a port, so by now, Didi could be on a boat sailing who knows where!"

1 ANDY STOLE THE MEGALAPTERYX SKELETON . . .

2 AND HE GAVE IT TO AN ACCOMPLICE!

"Wait a second," Charlotte said. "Tāmati, didn't you hear Andy say 'tomorrow afternoon at Bayswater'? We might still have time to find Didi!"

"Which means that we'll have to spend another night in the CAMPER," added Colette with a small sigh.

Nicky put her arm around her friend's shoulders as they walked back to the RV parked by the Waitomo caves. Then she murmured,

"Don't get down in the snout — we'll catch the thieves tomorrow. Before you know it, we'll be back at the Brown Farm, where you can have a long shower and time to style your fur!"

Colette sighed. "I'd love a shower, but I'd also love to **FIND** Didi."

"I have an idea," Tāmati said to them. "Since we have a little time, what do you say we stop in my hometown, Rotorua, for the night?"

"Is it nearby?" asked Pam.

"It's about two hours away," Tāmati said. "My grandma still lives there, and I'm sure she would be happy to host us."

"That's a fabumouse idea!" Pam squeaked. "Let's shake a tail and go!"

She **LEAPED** into the camper, and her friends soon followed.

A RESTORATIVE BREAK

A few hours and lots of chatter later, the group was approaching Rotorua. As they got closer, they started seeing some dense, low clouds filling the air.

"What are those?" Paulina asked.

"Rotorua is a geothermal area, which means there are geysers, bubbling mud pools, steaming vents, and natural hot springs that emit clouds of VAPOR!" Charlotte explained.

Tāmati nodded from the driver's seat. "And we'll get to my grandma's house in just a few minutes."

"Look!" exclaimed Colette, pointing out the window. A large pool of steaming water reflected the light of the setting sun.

Soon, the RV stopped in front of a small white house with a RED roof. Tāmati got out and knocked on the door.

An **elderly** mouse answered and lit up with a big smile when she saw who it was. "Tāmati!" she said.

"Grandma!" he cried. Then he explained the situation to her while his friends got out of the RV. His grandma nodded and turned toward the mouselets.

They were holding their **PAWS** out to shake, but instead, she touched each of their snouts and foreheads with her own in a very warm greeting.

"This greeting is called **hongi**," Charlotte explained quietly. "It's a traditional

Māori greeting, and demonstrates respect and hospitality."

Tāmati's grandma then asked the mice if they were tired or hungry.

"Actually, both!" Charlotte admitted.

"I will prepare a **special** meal for you," the elderly mouse responded. "And in the meantime, you can relax with a nice bath. What do you say?"

"Great idea — thank you!" Tāmati said.

"That sounds fabumouse, but do we really all have time for a bath?" Colette asked.

Tāmati chuckled. "We wouldn't if we were using a bathtub — but we have something much better in Rotorua!"

Without explaining more, Tāmati invited

his friends to change into swimsuits and follow him. They soon found themselves walking through a lush grove. They could smell moss and hear water gently lapping in the distance.

"Oooh!" the Thea Sisters exclaimed when they reached the end of the trail. It opened into a clearing where a small waterfall flowed down into a sparkling **pool**.

"Welcome to one of the local thermal pools! This water is naturally HOTTER than grilled cheese — see for yourself!" Tāmati said proudly.

"I won't take your squeak for it!" replied Pam, who dropped her things and jumped in with a huge splash onto her friends. They burst out laughing.

Colette rolled her eyes cheerfully, then

carefully tied up her fur before going in with the others.

Their unexpected natural bath was very pleasant, but short: The sun was beginning to set, and everyone's bellies were starting to grumble. The friends headed back to the house, then dried off and changed for dinner.

Soon they sat around the table in the small, welcoming kitchen.

"I hope you like this," Tāmati's grandma said as she set out a large variety of cooked vegetables and a delicious-looking meat stew. "I wanted you to try some typical Māori food. I cooked it using a traditional method called *hangi*, which uses heat from the earth."

"It's absolutely delicious," Pam said.

"How does it use the heat from the earth?" Paulina asked.

Tāmati's grandma responded, "The food is covered in wet cloths and cooked on top of heated stones in a pit in the ground for several

hours. Luckily, I prepared lots of food for a party just last night — so I won't leave you with empty stomachs!"

"It's marvemouse!" Violet said. "The bread is exquisite, too!"

"Chomp! Chomp!"

"It's called *rewena*," explained Tāmati. "The dough is made with flour, potato, and honey, or at least I think it is. Grandma won't give me her recipe!"

The elderly mouse smiled. "Everyone has their little **SECRETS**!"

After the delicious dinner, the Thea Sisters were ready to turn in.

"Thank you for the **hospitality**," Nicky said to Tāmati's grandmother.

"It's nothing! I know that you are special

mouselets — and my grandson told me you're on an important **mission**," she replied.

"Tāmati is right. We're hoping to complete it tomorrow!" Nicky said with a smile.

INVESTIGATION
AT THE PORT

The friends got up very early the next morning, gave a warm good-bye to Tāmati's grandmother, and left for Bayswater, a suburb of the city of Auckland, located on a peninsula in the bay.

"I can feel us getting closer to Didi!" Paulina said as she settled into the *driver's seat* of the RV. "What do you all think?"

But no one responded.

"Hello?" she said, turning around before starting the motor. "But . . . everyone's asleep?!"

The only response was a light SNORE from Pam, curled up in her seat. All the mouselets were sleeping deeply.

"I think this will be a long and silent trip, right, Tāmati?" Paulina said to the ratlet in the passenger's seat up front. But when she turned to look at him, he was sound **asleep**, too!

Paulina sighed and started the RV.

As she drove, her companions woke up one by one. They soon figured out their plan for the day: They would divide into groups to search the PORT for Didi.

"Park down there," Charlotte advised when they reached Bayswater, pointing at a side street close to the port.

Before they split up, Nicky reminded her

FRIENDS, "See you at the main dock in forty-five minutes, okay?"

Everyone nodded and set off. Pam, Paulina, and Charlotte **SEARCHED** the area away from the water. Colette and Violet looked at buildings near the port. Nicky and Tāmati scoured the wharf, where yachts and boats were docked.

"There are too many boats," Tāmati said. "I'll check for any strange movements on this side and you check the other?"

Nicky nodded. "Good idea. Let's meet back here in half an hour."

"Perfect!" the ratlet said, and set off along the pier.

Forty-five minutes later, the mice gathered at the main dock.

"Did you find anything, sisters?" Pam asked Colette and Violet.

"No," Violet replied. "It was very quiet, and we didn't see the slightest trace of Didi."

There was no trace . . .

Did you find anything?

"Us either." Charlotte sighed. "It's really hard to search without any sort of precise **CLUE** to follow . . ."

Just then Tāmati arrived.

Here I am, mouselets!

"Tāmati, do you have any good news?" Colette asked.

He shook his snout. "No. We split up, and I didn't find anything. I don't know about Nicky — I **THOUGHT** she'd already be here!"

"No, we haven't seen her," Paulina said.

Tāmati frowned. "We'd agreed to meet up after half an hour, but she didn't show, so I figured she had come directly to you mice."

"We'd better go to *LOOK* for her, then," replied Paulina, a little worried.

Bzzz, bzzz! Bzzz, bzzz!

"Nicky just sent a message!" Colette squeaked, showing them her MousePhone.

Mouselets, I think I finally found Didi!

A MYSTERIOUS BAG

Nicky looked around.

Some time had passed since she'd jumped aboard the small yacht just before it set out to sea. She was hidden behind a few wooden crates in the hold, thinking about what to do next.

The hold was quite *MESSY.* There were ropes, old cartons, piles of boxes, and junk everywhere.

Under a shelf, however, Nicky finally caught a glimpse of something interesting: a black bag that looked like the one she remembered Andy carrying the night that he **stayed** at the Brown Farm.

That was why she'd gotten onto the boat — she'd seen a rat loading the bag. Could it have something to do with the missing skeleton? She wanted to ask someone about it, so she made her way into the hold. But before she could find anyone, the boat had taken off — and she had no idea where it was going.

Luckily, she had her phone with her, so she'd texted her friends to let them know where she had gone.

As Nicky approached the bag, she saw that it had a logo of an anchor and two fish on it, exactly like Andy's. It had to be the same bag!

Her heart was pounding. Just as she was going to open the bag . . . SKREEEEAK!

A loud creak from behind her made her jump, and she hid again behind some crates.

But nothing happened. She was just about to come out when muffled movements and noises from the deck above told her that the boat was about to dock.

Nicky tried to imagine what her friends would do: Colette would stay calm, and Violet would take a deep breath and think. After a moment of calm thought, Nicky jumped out in a flash and slipped her **phone** into one of the bag's pockets, then went back to her hiding place.

She curled up as small as possible and tried to stay silent as pawsteps **RAN** down the ladder to the hold.

Done!

"Let's take it away!" a sharp masculine squeak ordered. Several mice thumped around, moving crates and dragging away something heavy.

"Careful!" one of them said. "It's very special and fragile!"

"We're almost there," said another. "This nice bag comes with us. We'll bring it to safety . . . under the lava!"

Then everything got quiet.

Nicky stayed still for a few more minutes to be sure they were gone, then crept up to the deck and made her way off the yacht. She found herself on a green island in crystal-clear waters.

It was a gorgeous view, but she felt like she'd swallowed a cheese wheel whole. She was alone, in an unknown location. She hoped with all her heart that she'd done the right thing to **FiND** Didi.

CLUE!

DOES ANDY'S BAG CONTAIN THE MEGALAPTERYX SKELETON? WHO TOOK IT OFF THE BOAT — AND WHERE ARE THEY DOCKED?

A FAMILIAR RINGTONE

Nicky had just taken a few uncertain steps down the dock when she heard a familiar cry. "**NICKY!**"

She spun around and saw her friends on a nearby pier! They were *RUNNING* to meet her, yelling, "Are you okay?"

Before she could respond, Pam was squeezing her in a tight hu9. "I knew that you could do it — but you made us worried!"

Soon the whole group was there, squeaking all at once.

"How did you get on the boat?"

"Did you see who was driving?"

"Did you DiSCoveR something about Didi?"

Nicky looked at her friends in shock. "I'll

tell you everything," she said. "But first tell me how you FOUND me! And also . . . where are we?!"

Colette explained, "Paulina was so great. She tracked your phone's GPS and saw that you were sailing toward Rangitoto!"

"Rangitoto?" repeated Nicky.

"It's the name of the VOLCANIC island we're on," Tāmati explained.

Then Nicky told them, "I don't know why the boat came here, but I'm almost sure that Didi was on board: I saw Andy's bag! Some mice took it off here."

"Did you see where they went?" Colette asked.

Nicky shook her snout. "Unfortunately not." Her friends looked disappointed, but she continued. "Don't worry — I actually had the same IDEA as Paulina!"

"What do you mean?" Pam asked.

"I put my MousePhone into a pocket of the bag," Nicky said with a grin.

"So if we follow the signal of your PHONE, we'll find Didi!" Tāmati concluded, hugging her. "Great job!"

"Fantastic! Just give me a second," said Paulina, fumbling with her tablet. "It looks like Didi is climbing toward the top of the crater!"

"I bet we're in for a STEEP hike!" Pam exclaimed.

"I'm afraid so," Charlotte said. "But we seem close to the finish line!"

Nicky nodded. "I think we are — I heard

Let's see . . .

the mice say they would take the bag 'under the lava,' so the crater of a volcano makes sense."

Paulina started walking toward where her tablet said Nicky's phone was, and everyone followed.

"It seems like they stop every so often," Paulina said.

"Well, even if Didi is small, I think it's still pretty **HEAVY**. They may be stopping to rest," Tāmati said.

The friends' chatter was soon replaced by the rhythm of hiking as the **summit** of the crater grew closer.

The land around them alternated between the intense green forest and the dark gray lava stone.

"We've reached the PHONE," Paulina announced. "Didi must be somewhere around here."

"Right here?" Pam asked, skeptical. They were by a

WOODEN walkway that led to a small viewing platform, where two female mice were admiring the *landscape*.

"Are you sure it's this spot exactly?" Colette asked. "There are only *tourists* here."

"Yes, I'm certain — the GPS signal brought us right here," confirmed Paulina. "It's very accurate."

"But the bag isn't here," said Nicky, perplexed. "Unless it's hidden it in a bush nearby . . . or maybe underground?"

"I know how to check!" Violet said. "Colette, call Nicky's phone. We'll hear if it rings, and where!"

Huh?!

Colette did so, and they heard a familiar **ringtone** from one of the two tourists!

The mouse looked around her, then realized that the ring came from her own purse. With great surprise, she found Nicky's cell phone.

"This isn't mine! How did it wind

up in here?!" she wondered aloud.

"Excuse me, ma'am — that's actually my phone," Nicky said, approaching her. "I don't know how, but it must have wound up in your purse by **mistake**!"

"But — how . . . ?" she spluttered in confusion.

"Come on, Mary, let's not make a big deal about it," said the other tourist. "It could have happened during the ferry ride — there were all those big waves!"

Mary nodded. "You're right, Edwige!" Then she turned to Nicky and gave back the phone with a smile. "It must have happened as my friend said: that we were close by during the crossing and with all that movement, it slipped into my bag!"

Nicky nodded and thanked her. Back with her friends, she whispered in disappointment, "I guess the **thief** must have noticed my trick and tossed my phone in that mouse's bag to throw us off his trail."

"It's okay, Nicky," Paulina said. "It was a good idea. And if it weren't for you, we wouldn't have gotten this far."

"Yeah!" Tāmati agreed. "Didi is somewhere on this island, and we will find it!"

nothing is lost

Now that they had the phone, going farther toward the crater didn't make sense. So the friends turned around and went back toward the dock.

"Maybe we can split up again," Colette said. "How big is this island?"

Paulina stopped for a moment to look ONLINE and said, "It's big, but there aren't that many roads. We could look at the **MAP** and come up with a plan to search them."

"Let's hurry to go back down, then," Nicky said. "At the very least, we can check to see if the boat I was on is still there."

"If it is, we still have a chance to find and CATCH the rat who brought Didi here!" Tāmati exclaimed.

The mice soon arrived back at the harbor.

"There it is! It's still here!" Nicky cried, pointing at the yacht that she'd hidden on.

"Great! Let's stay here and wait for the **CREW** to come back on board," Violet said.

"Okay, let's go — **hey!**" Pam squeaked,

tripping over something. "What's this?" She bent down and picked up a small, battered **flashlight** from the ground near the boat. She tried to turn it on, but, "It doesn't work!" she announced.

"Just leave it, Pam," Paulina said. "We'll find a quiet place to wait."

The boat is down there!

Pam was about to throw away the flashlight, but something caught her attention. "Cheese and crackers! This has the LOGO for Abel Tasman National Park on it!"

"Can I see?" asked Tāmati, taking the flashlight. "You're right . . . this can't be a COINCIDENCE!"

"Are you thinking what I'm thinking?" Charlotte asked her friends.

Everyone nodded.

"**Dr. Sinclair** must be here!" Violet said. "When he got off the yacht with the bag that Didi is in, he must've had this flashlight as well — but when he realized it didn't work, he **left** it here on the dock."

"Maybe so, but why would he need a flashlight in full daylight?" Colette asked.

Paulina smiled. "I read some information while I was looking up Rangitoto, and I know how a flashlight can help around here: to light up the **lava caves** under the volcano!"

Nicky clapped a paw to her snout. "Crusty cheddar, of course! When that rat on the boat said that he would put the bag 'under the lava,' he meant in the **caves** formed by lava!"

"Let's go there right now!" Charlotte squeaked.

"Yes, let's hurry!" Paulina said. "But I have some bad news. We'll have to climb back up part of the way we just came down."

Pam sighed. "This time, we better find Didi. I don't

Crusty cheddar!

know how much farther I can go without a
SNACK!"

Tāmati rummaged in his backpack and
pawed Pam a dried fruit bar. "Could this
work? It should give you a little bit of
energy."

"**THANKS!** I think I can last another half hour with this," Pam replied, and the others burst out laughing.

LET'S REVIEW THE CLUES!

THE FRIENDS TRACKED THE SIGNAL OF NICKY'S PHONE AND ENDED UP NEAR THE CRATER — BUT THEY DISCOVERED HER PHONE WAS HIDDEN IN A TOURIST'S PURSE INSTEAD OF ANDY'S BAG.

NEAR THE BOAT THAT BROUGHT OVER NICKY AND THE BAG, THERE WAS A FLASHLIGHT WITH THE LOGO OF THE ABEL TASMAN NATIONAL PARK. IT'S POSSIBLE THAT DR. SINCLAIR LOST IT OR THREW IT OUT!

IT SEEMS LIKE DR. SINCLAIR IS NOW TAKING DIDI "UNDER THE LAVA" TO THE ISLAND'S LAVA CAVES!

THE LAST STEP

While the friends hurried toward their new goal, Paulina said, "There are several lava caves here in Rangitoto. It will take some time, but if we divide up and each explore a different one, we should be able to find Didi!"

Nicky agreed. "That sounds like the fastest option. If Sinclair has hidden Didi there, he won't be able to ESCAPE us!"

We'll find it!

"The first mouse to DISCOVER something should text everyone so that we can **meet** back up and take Sinclair down!" Colette said.

The friends agreed. "Let's go!"

Tāmati set out for the farthest cave. There, he ran into a group of noisy tourists, which made his **mission** harder than he'd hoped.

Meanwhile, Pam, Colette, and Paulina explored the three closest caves without finding any **CLUES**.

Charlotte and Nicky went to two caves not far away. Neither was very large, and they were both packed with tourists.

Violet headed to a smaller, quieter **CAVE** that was not visited much.

Before going in, she observed the entrance carefully and noticed some clues: broken **twigs**, a few overturned stones, and a light track on the ground, as if someone had dragged something heavy inside.

The mouselet gathered her courage and looked at the cave's dark entrance. She was almost certain that Didi was in there, so she MESSAGED her friends to verify that no one else had found any interesting clues.

Everyone responded as she had expected. So Violet texted them, "Meet me here — this must be the cave!"

In a few minutes, her friends began to arrive. When the whole group was together, waiting quietly, Violet gave a nod and led them into the **CAVE**.

For the first few seconds, everyone's eyes had to adjust to the **darkness** inside. They turned on the flashlights they had in their backpacks and shone them at the rock walls.

"Careful where you put your feet," Tāmati said, and gave Nicky a paw to help her forward in the darkness. "The ground can be uneven or wet down here."

They soon reached the end of the cave — and found nothing but rock, roots, and dirt.

"Vi, there's **NOTHING** here," Paulina said quietly.

"Let's be sure to check everywhere," Tāmati added.

Colette pointed at a spot along the wall. "Look, it seems like the rocks over there have been moved!"

Nicky immediately lit up the spot with a flashlight.

"It's here!"

Everyone SCURRIED over and saw the dark bag with the logo of an anchor and two fish.

Without squeaking a word, the friends took the bag from its **hiding** place and brought it outside very carefully.

The SUNLIGHT dazzled them for a moment, and then Nicky began to gently open the bag. Inside, there was a pile of paper and foam. **Underneath** they found . . . Didi!

Tāmati was beside himself with joy as he examined the PRECIOUS artifact that they'd finally found. His voice trembling with emotion, he confirmed, "It's definitely the *Megalapteryx*! I can't believe it!"

The mouselets high-fived one another. But the excitement the friends felt for having completed their mission did not last long.

"**PAWS OFF!**" a sharp squeak ordered.

PLOT TWIST

The Thea Sisters and their friends froze. A few feet away from them, standing among the rocks, was **Dr. Sinclair**! Even though he wore hiking clothes and no lab coat, the mice immediately recognized him from the photo in Andy's mint tin.

"Andy warned me about a bunch of **nosy** rodents going around and asking questions," he said. "I admit that you've been clever to get this far, but now it's time for you to let go of my skeleton and get out of the way."

"Leave Didi alone!" Pam shouted, jumping in front of

the bag to defend the precious bones.

Sinclair looked surprised, then broke into a mocking laugh. "You even gave it a name — how cute! If you leave now without making a fuss, no one will get hurt. I'll finish my job, and you can all go home in peace."

Tāmati took a step forward. "If you think that we'll let you keep the *Megalapteryx didinus*, you are very wrong," he declared. "It is an ARTiFACT of enormouse importance, and it belongs back at Te Papa in Wellington!"

"You're RIGHT, you know?" Sinclair responded. "It's of enormouse importance . . . and enormouse value! There is a **collector** eager to get hold of it, and he'll be here very soon to buy it from me. Everything has been planned in perfect detail: That cheesebrain

Andy **STOLE** the skeleton, then gave it to me. I verified it was all there and brought it to this **unlikely** place to store it and wait for the buyer to collect it! Only *you* weren't expected, so you need to go away **NOW**!"

"Will the buyer arrive by boat?" Paulina asked.

Sinclair was surprised by the sudden question and replied, "Obviously. In fact, his **YACHT** should be docking in Rangitoto now. It won't draw attention in such a touristy place — which was my idea, of course! But enough of this. You must —"

"I wonder what kind of rodent collects **extinct** animals," Paulina went on. "And how did he find you, Dr. Sinclair, an unsuspecting **SCIENTIST** who works with

Abel Tasman National Park, and Andy, a seemingly harmless tour guide from Waitomo . . ."

Sinclair sneered, "What is all this chatter? Do you think you're some kind of **detective**?"

"We all are, actually," Colette said, smiling.

"It's too bad that no one would take you seriously," the doctor scoffed. "Your time to play detectives is over. We can do this the hard way." He moved toward Tāmati **THREATENINGLY.**

"Don't you dare touch any of us!" Tāmati cried.

"It's okay, Tāmati," Paulina said. "We'll just leave."

Everyone turned to her in shock.

"But we can't let him take Didi!" Pam objected.

Paulina, however, smiled and kept squeaking. "Don't worry! No one's getting far away with Didi." Then she brought out her paw from behind her back. She was holding her tablet. "A few minutes ago, I made an emergency call to the POLICE, and they've heard enough detail to arrest the thieves and bring the skeleton to safety. Right, officers?"

"Affirmative! We just sent a patrol to the site!" the squeak of a policeman confirmed **loud** and clear through the tablet.

Dr. Sinclair turned as pale as mozzarella. He moved toward Tāmati, but Nicky **BLOCKED** him.

"That's not a wise choice, Dr. Sinclair. Don't make your situation any worse," the mouselet **WARNED** him in a serious squeak.

The doctor hesitated, then turned on his heel and fled.

"LET HIM GO," Paulina said. "We have what we came for. The police will find him. The important thing is we have Didi!"

GOOD-BYE

Everything went exactly according to Paulina's plan. The POLICE were able to catch both Dr. Sinclair and the collector who hired him and Andy for the **theft** — and they launched an investigation into what else the collector had been stealing.

Get in!

Didi was brought carefully back to Wellington, where the Museum of New Zealand Te Papa Tongarewa welcomed it with great joy.

"It was really a fabumouse adventure," Paulina declared with a big sigh as she closed her Suitcase back at the Brown Farm.

"You can squeak that again!" Pam agreed. "Clues, chases, exploring parks and ports, and so many caves!"

Just then the unmistakable horn of the RV filled the air: BEEEEP! BEEEEP!

"That's Charlotte — let's go!" Nicky exclaimed.

The Thea Sisters said a warm good-bye to **Mr. Brown** and went to load their luggage into the camper.

"Where's Coco?" asked Violet, looking around.

"It's been a while since she DISAPPEARED, actually," Paulina said. "I'll go see if she's still in the bedroom." A few seconds later, Paulina came back outside. "She's not there!"

"Where could she be? We're going to be late." Charlotte sighed.

"Wait, I might know where she is!" Pam cried. She hurried toward the **chicken coop**. "Colette, are you here?"

Colette appeared in the doorway — with the little hen **DOROTHY** in her paws!

"Sorry, I had say good-bye to my little friend!" Colette smiled.

The others burst into laughter.

Finally, they were ready to leave.

"We'll be there in time for the party, right?" Nicky asked anxiously once the RV started moving.

"Absolutely!" Charlotte said. "And Tāmati assured us that they wouldn't start without us!"

"I'm so happy that the mouseum gave us the REWARD for finding Didi," Paulina said.

Nicky nodded. "Now Tāmati can open the school that he's dreamed about, to teach art and design to the mouselings of Rotorua!"

"Do you think there will be some food cooked in a pit today?" asked Pam. "I'd love to have some more of that before leaving New Zealand!"

"Yes, there will be!" Charlotte said, laughing.

Time passed quickly on their drive. The Thea Sisters soon had to leave New Zealand and their dear friend Charlotte, but they were making the most of their last day. What better way to spend it than a party to celebrate Tāmati's school project?

Once they reached Rotorua, it wasn't hard to find the party: It seemed like the whole neighborhood was gathered at the center of the Marae, the meeting ground for the Māori community. The main building was decorated with beautiful carvings, and the atmosphere was festive. There was music, children playing, food, and cheerful chatter.

"Look, there's Tāmati!" said Pam, pointing.

"Cheese niblets, what is he **wearing**?!"

"It's a traditional MĀORI outfit!" replied Nicky, admiring Tāmati's kilt and the curving DESIGN on his torso.

"There you are!" the ratlet welcomed them happily. "Do you want to join the dance? I'll teach you the steps!"

And so the Thea Sisters and Charlotte found themselves involved in a very **FUN** traditional dance. They did their best to imitate the steps!

"I'm exhausted!" Nicky said at the end, dropping onto a bench.

Tāmati came up to her, smiling. "You were marvemouse!"

The two sat for a moment in SILENCE, and then both started squeaking at the same time.

"I'm so happy about your school —" Nicky began.

"I'm **sorry** you're leaving —" Tāmati said at the same time.

They both laughed.

It's super fun!

"You go first," Nicky said.

Tāmati gave her one of his big SMiLeS. "I'm sad that our time together was so short."

"Oh, but we can email, text, and video chat! You should come visit us on **Whale Island** with Charlotte someday!"

Tāmati nodded. "I would like that a lot! For now, though, I would like to give you this." He dropped a small object into Nicky's palm.

"It's your hei matau! Are you sure you want me to have it?"

"Yes, I'm sure," Tāmati said. "It can be a reminder of our **friendship** — and of your time here!"

Nicky smiled at him and, holding paws, they both turned their gaze upward . . .

TO NEW ZEALAND'S STARRY SKY!

I won't forget you!

Thea Stilton

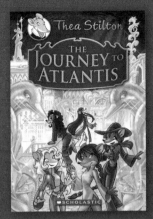

Special Editions

Don't miss any of these exciting series featuring the Thea Sisters!

Treasure Seekers

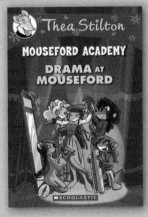

Mouseford Academy

Don't miss any of these exciting Thea Sisters adventures!

Thea Stilton and the Dragon's Code

Thea Stilton and the Mountain of Fire

Thea Stilton and the Ghost of the Shipwreck

Thea Stilton and the Secret City

Thea Stilton and the Mystery in Paris

Thea Stilton and the Cherry Blossom Adventure

Thea Stilton and the Star Castaways

Thea Stilton: Big Trouble in the Big Apple

Thea Stilton and the Ice Treasure

Thea Stilton and the Secret of the Old Castle

Thea Stilton and the Blue Scarab Hunt

Thea Stilton and the Prince's Emerald

Thea Stilton and the Mystery on the Orient Express

Thea Stilton and the Dancing Shadows

Thea Stilton and the Legend of the Fire Flowers

Thea Stilton and the Spanish Dance Mission